Matilda Jane

STORY BY JEAN GERRARD
PICTURES BY ROY GERRARD

FARRAR · STRAUS · GIROUX
NEW YORK

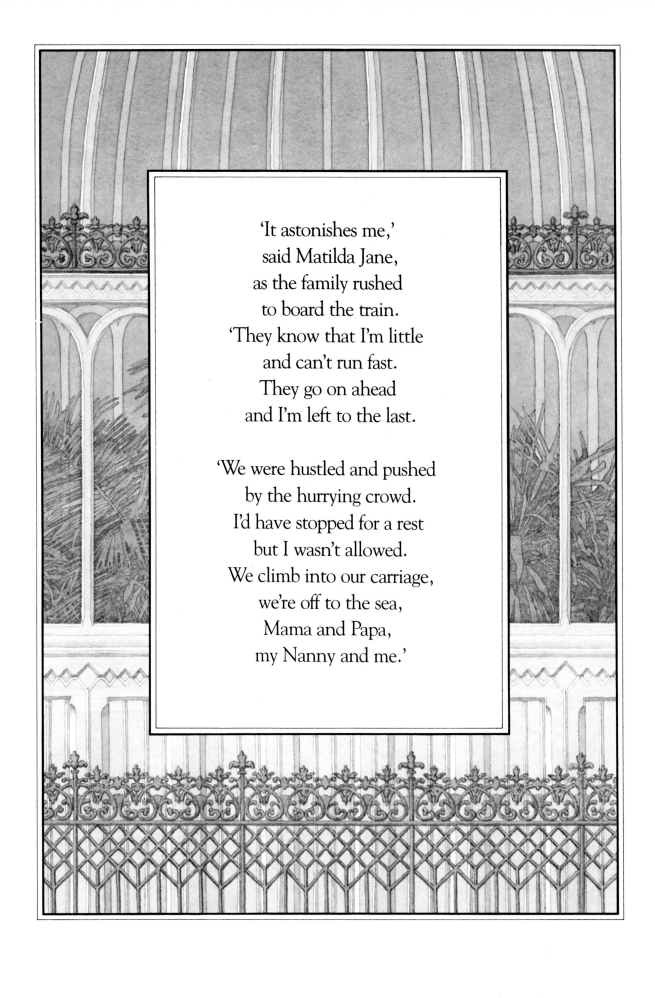

'It astonishes me,'
said Matilda Jane,
as the family rushed
to board the train.
'They know that I'm little
and can't run fast.
They go on ahead
and I'm left to the last.

'We were hustled and pushed
by the hurrying crowd.
I'd have stopped for a rest
but I wasn't allowed.
We climb into our carriage,
we're off to the sea,
Mama and Papa,
my Nanny and me.'

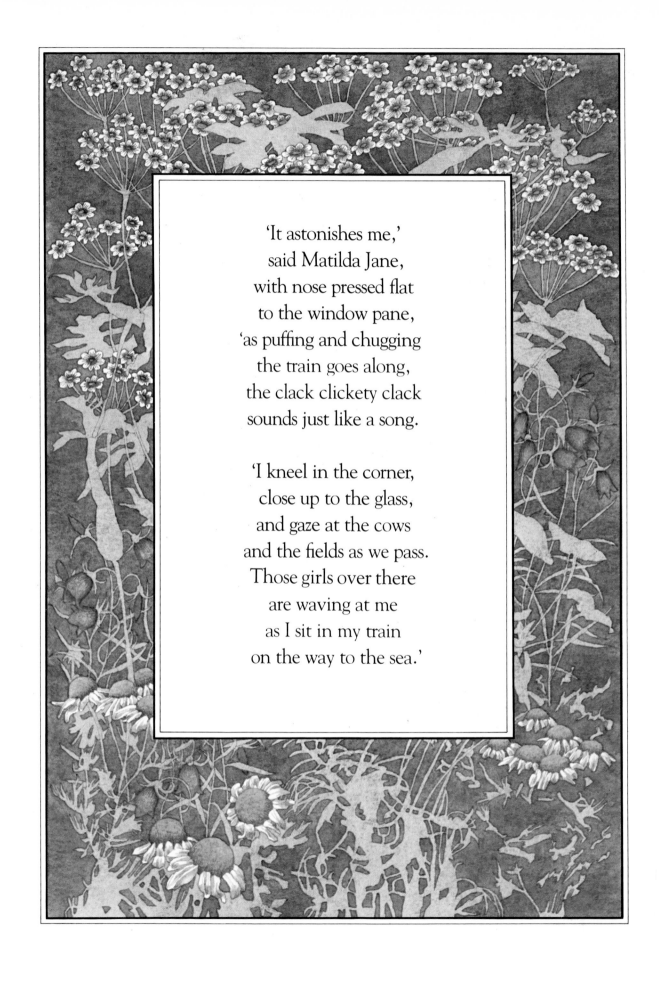

'It astonishes me,'
said Matilda Jane,
with nose pressed flat
to the window pane,
'as puffing and chugging
the train goes along,
the clack clickety clack
sounds just like a song.

'I kneel in the corner,
close up to the glass,
and gaze at the cows
and the fields as we pass.
Those girls over there
are waving at me
as I sit in my train
on the way to the sea.'

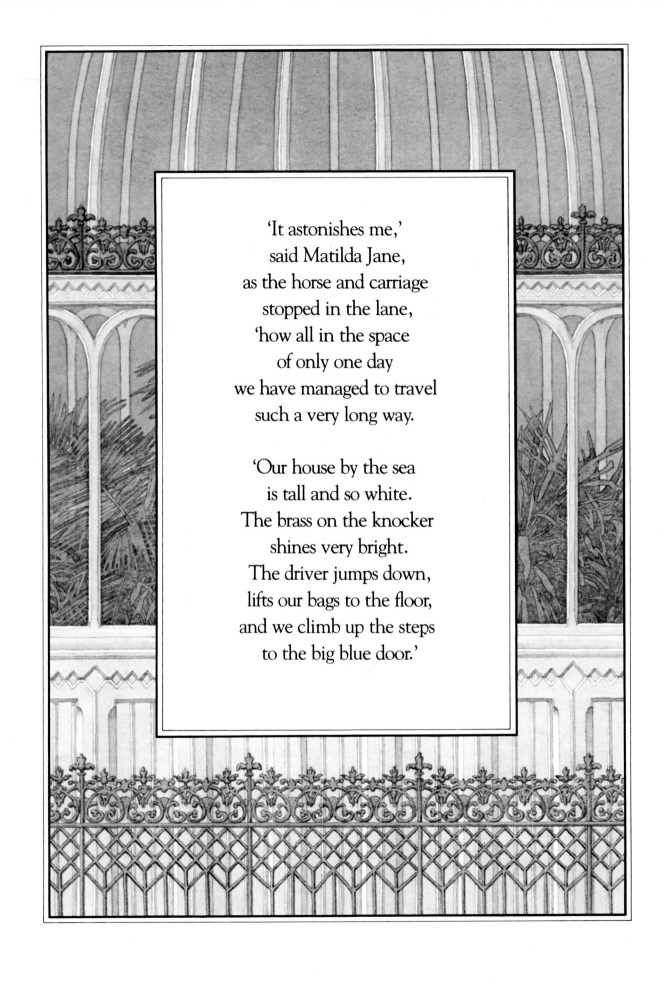

'It astonishes me,'
said Matilda Jane,
as the horse and carriage
stopped in the lane,
'how all in the space
of only one day
we have managed to travel
such a very long way.

'Our house by the sea
is tall and so white.
The brass on the knocker
shines very bright.
The driver jumps down,
lifts our bags to the floor,
and we climb up the steps
to the big blue door.'

Matilda Jane
was astonished to see
that Mrs Jones
had made their tea.
How did she know
they were going to arrive
right on the dot
of half-past five?

There was cake and jam
and toasted bread.
'There's plenty more,'
the landlady said.
Then a walk on the prom
till half-past eight.
Matilda had never
been up so late.

'It astonishes me,'
said Matilda next day
as they sat on the beach
and looked out at the bay.
'I wonder wherever
the waves can come from?
They sometimes come rolling
right up to the prom.

'It's exceedingly strange
that they all go away.
It seems that they do it
most every day.
I think when they go
it's ever so grand
for then we can play
again on the sand.'

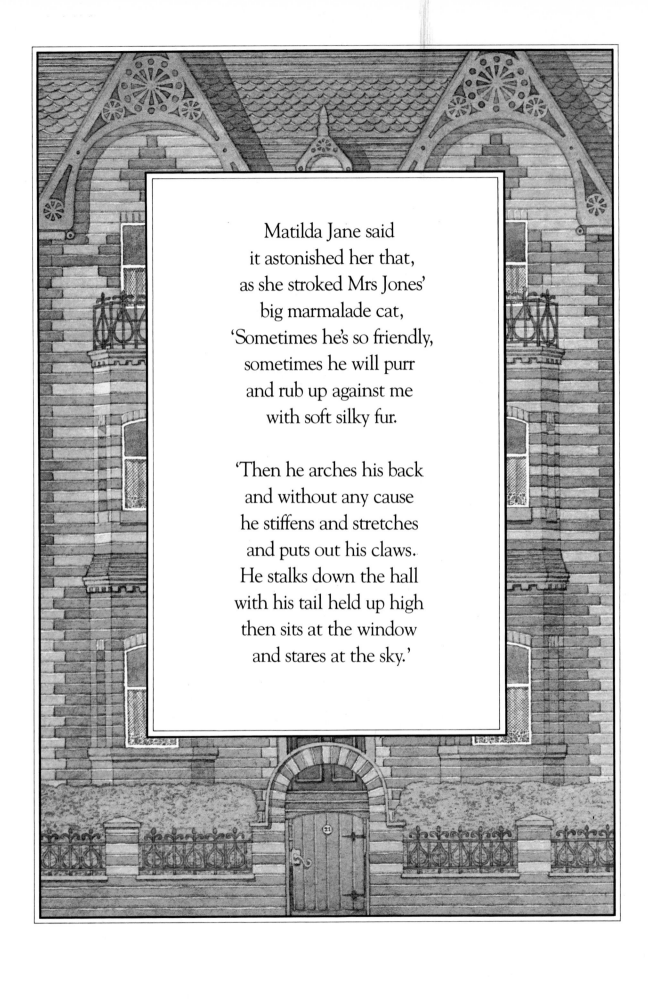

Matilda Jane said
it astonished her that,
as she stroked Mrs Jones'
big marmalade cat,
'Sometimes he's so friendly,
sometimes he will purr
and rub up against me
with soft silky fur.

'Then he arches his back
and without any cause
he stiffens and stretches
and puts out his claws.
He stalks down the hall
with his tail held up high
then sits at the window
and stares at the sky.'

'It astonishes me,'
said Matilda with glee,
'the way grown-ups look
when they enter the sea.
With their trousers rolled up
and their skirts held high,
it's hard not to smile
or to laugh, but I'll try.

'There are bathing machines
at the edge of the sea.
We walk down the steps,
both my Nanny and me.
I paddle my toes
as the ripples come in,
then go into the water
right up to my chin.'

'It astonishes me,'
Matilda Jane thought,
'that though hundreds and hundreds
of fish have been caught,
there seem to be heaps
every day, just the same –
in fact, quite as many
as when we first came.

'Where do they all come from?
Where do they all go?
I asked an old fisherman,
but he didn't know.
He said they're from China
or even Peru.
Somehow I don't think
that his stories are true.'

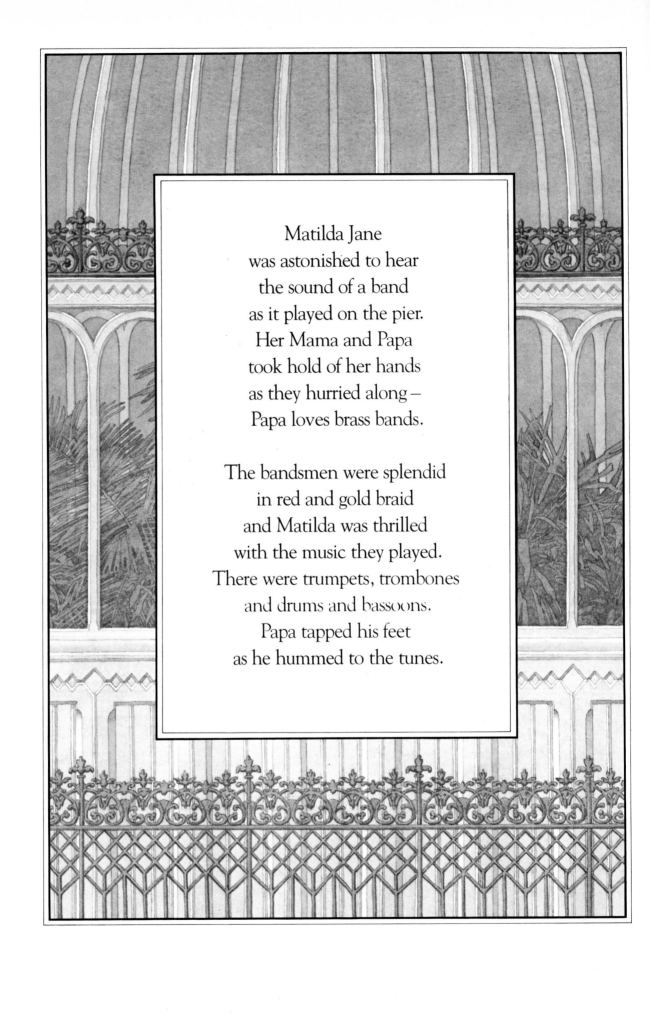

Matilda Jane
was astonished to hear
the sound of a band
as it played on the pier.
Her Mama and Papa
took hold of her hands
as they hurried along –
Papa loves brass bands.

The bandsmen were splendid
in red and gold braid
and Matilda was thrilled
with the music they played.
There were trumpets, trombones
and drums and bassoons.
Papa tapped his feet
as he hummed to the tunes.

'It astonishes me,'
Matilda Jane sighed
as she stood on the pier
and looked over the side.
'My Nanny says mermaids
live deep down below,
but we never can see them,
so how does she know?

'She says that they live
way down with the fish,
and no matter how much
I dream and I wish,
they will never come up
to be seen from the land.
Why are they so shy?
I just don't understand.'

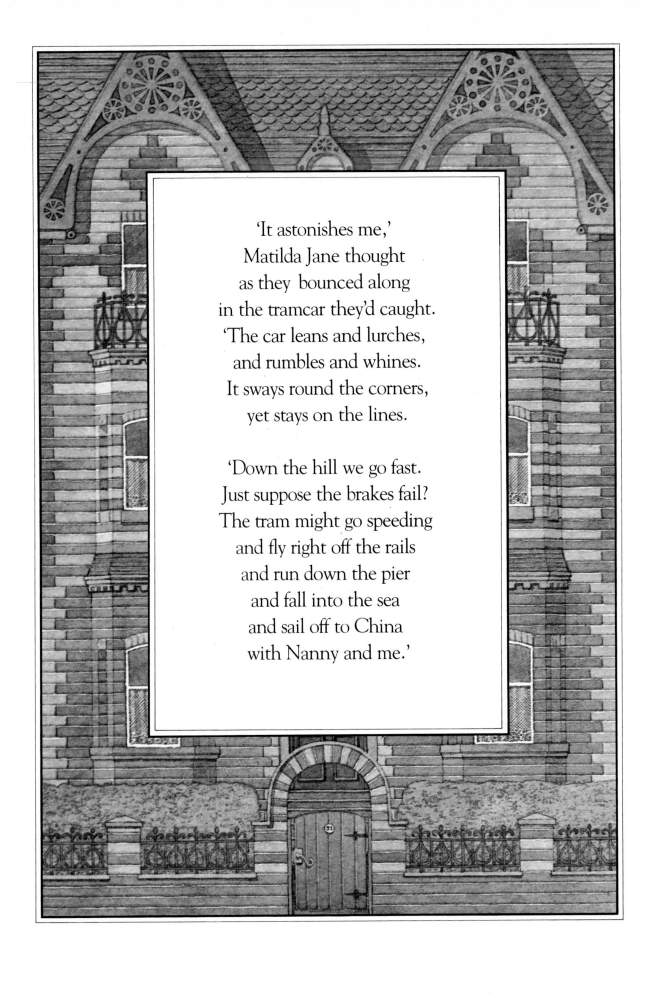

'It astonishes me,'
Matilda Jane thought
as they bounced along
in the tramcar they'd caught.
'The car leans and lurches,
and rumbles and whines.
It sways round the corners,
yet stays on the lines.

'Down the hill we go fast.
Just suppose the brakes fail?
The tram might go speeding
and fly right off the rails
and run down the pier
and fall into the sea
and sail off to China
with Nanny and me.'

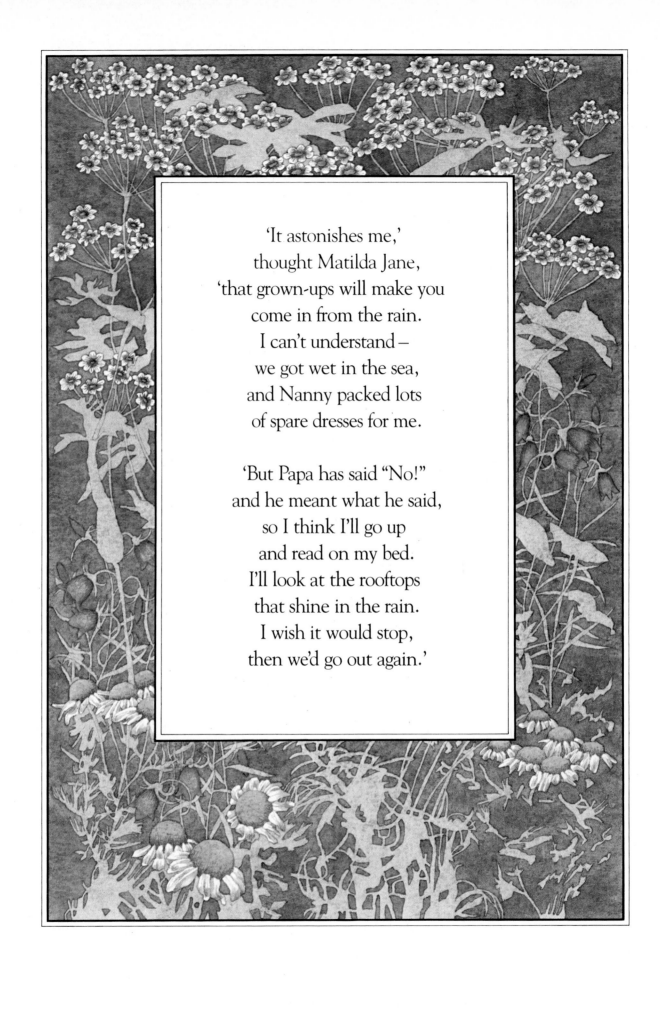

'It astonishes me,'
thought Matilda Jane,
'that grown-ups will make you
come in from the rain.
I can't understand –
we got wet in the sea,
and Nanny packed lots
of spare dresses for me.

'But Papa has said "No!"
and he meant what he said,
so I think I'll go up
and read on my bed.
I'll look at the rooftops
that shine in the rain.
I wish it would stop,
then we'd go out again.'

'It astonishes me,'
said Matilda with sorrow,
'that, alas, we shall all
be back home by tomorrow.
It doesn't seem long
since we came on the train.
It will be a whole year
till we come here again.

'Goodbye to the pier
and the sea and the sand.
And the marmalade cat
and the jolly brass band.
How time seemed to fly
with the things that we've done
and the places we've seen –
Oh, it has been fun!'

'It astonishes me,'
Matilda Jane grumbled
as out of her bed
the next morning she tumbled.
'They've packed all the cases,
they're ready to go.
I'm hardly awake
but they say that I'm slow.

'Now Mrs Jones waves
as we leave for the train
and she says she'll be happy
to see us again.
I thought yesterday
that to leave would be sad,
but today, travelling home,
I'm really quite glad.'

'It astonishes me,'
Matilda Jane said
when she'd finished her prayers
and jumped into her bed,
'that the moon that is shining
at home upon me
is the same moon that's shining
right down on the sea.

'It's nice to be back
in my own little bed,
with thoughts of the seaside
going round in my head.
I remember the seaweed,
the shells and the foam.
It was grand at the sea,
but I'm glad that I'm home.'